James A. Froude

Poems by Zeta

James A. Froude

Poems by Zeta

ISBN/EAN: 9783337158460

Printed in Europe, USA, Canada, Australia, Japan

Cover: Foto ©Andreas Hilbeck / pixelio.de

More available books at **www.hansebooks.com**

POEMS.

POEMS.

BY

ZETA.

"—— Explebo numerum reddarque tenebris."—Virgil.

LONDON:

CHARLES WESTERTON,

27, ST. GEORGE'S PLACE, HYDE PARK CORNER.

——

1871.

CONTENTS.

—◆—

FADING FLOWERS.

WHERE late in simple guise ye gladly
   grew,
   Why have I torn you from the earth ye
   flowers ?
   Why robb'd you of your life, more sweet than
   ours,
More fairly dealt and more to Nature true ?
And odours indrawn from the breath of heaven,
   And freshness from the falling tears of Night,
   And forms of loveliness and hues of light,
My ruthless hands to stay in vain were given !

B

Yes, I have doomed you for my selfish sense.

   The fragrance of your life is dying fast,

   Faint, as the memory of the happy past.

So, from the heart which trusts in innocence,

Man tears the sweets, then leaves it to decay,

With—like these flowers—its virtue passed away.

AN ADDRESS TO BEN LOMOND.

(Lines written at Tarbet.)

—◆—

HOU guardian of the mighty lake!
  Around whose base the dark waves
  break ;
I muse upon thy lonely strand,
A stranger from a distant land.
I hear thy waters sadly fall,
Wailing within their prison wall ;
Whilst the night-winds in sighs impart
Their solemn music to my heart.
And here, beneath the spanning heaven,
That temple God to all has given,

I breathe a prayer, my life may be,
In its bold outline, like to thee ;
Yet that some influence from above
May smooth its harshness into love ;
Still keeping with that softer hue
The stamp of Nature fresh and true.
So that it may, when wrongs abound,
In all its native force be found,
Each sterner feature bring to light,
And start, in grandeur, on the sight.
And thus may years upon me come,
Till the deep shadows of the tomb,
Stealing like mists around thy head,
Enrol me with the silent dead.

SOROR SOLA.

NE sharp cry, one weak convulsion,
  One faint clinging, in thy pain,
  Closer to the heart that loved thee
   Dearly, dearly, but in vain.
And all is hush'd to rest within thee,
  Death's strange cloud hath left thy face ;
Thine arms hang loose which late around me
  Tightened for a last embrace.
Come ! I'll lay thee on the pillow,
  Which thy cheek with mine hath press'd,
For I could not bear to feel thee,
  Growing cold upon my breast.
Where thou, where thou, would'st sink to slumber,
  Still as came the evening chime,

When thy day with dark was ended,
  In the happy olden time.
Thou wert young to die, my brother,
  O ! too young, but now 'tis past ;
Thou hast followed thy sweet mother,
  Through the gates of death at last.
When she died, she bade me guard thee,
  And I watch'd thee long and well ;
But something which I could not master
  On thy youthful spirit fell.
Farewell ! I pray'd to heaven to spare thee,
  Thou wert purer than my prayer ;
Ere thy form is cold beside me,
  Shall the soul I loved be there.
There, if ever I may join thee,
  We shall meet again, my boy ;
With the others I remember,
  Dwelling in eternal joy.

THE SLAVE.

THERE came from out a kindred land,
 Far by the western wave,
A pleader for a wretched race,
 A fugitive, a slave.

He bore the dark and fatal hue,
 The great God gave his kind,
The God who made him dark, but left
 No darkness on his mind.

And on his skin a mark, a mark
 God doom'd him not to bear,
Which, with the lash's sounding coil,
 The freeman planted there.

In that land he sought his freedom,
　　But its blessings never knew,
For to him, like a curse, had clung
　　His heaven-allotted hue.

So he crossed the roaring ocean-gulf,
　　The dark and restless wave ;
And buried in its heaving breast
　　The heart-chains of the slave.

Pacing, pacing, the narrow deck,
　　Straining, with earnest gaze,
To catch the first ·faint streak of land,
　　Amidst the purpling haze.

Watching the steady compass point,
　　Saying, " It will be there,
The land I've dreamed of in my dreams,
　　And pray'd for in my prayer.

" The shore of merry England,
    That rock amidst the sea,
Where fearless men have sounded long
    The clarion of the free.

" Above her hangs the curling mist,
    About the wild wind blows ;
But strong beneath her stormy sky,
    The tree of freedom grows."

So he came to us and call'd around
    The beautiful, the good,
And proudly in the midst of them
    To tell his tale he stood.

He stood erect, as man should stand,
    The words of Truth to speak ;
The warm blood mounting from his heart
    To his worn and dusky cheek.

A silence, as of death, has bound
    That hall where thousands thronged ;
And darker seem'd the day to fall,
    In the presence of the wronged.

He stood, but from his parted lips
    No mournful story fell ;
For the struggling passions in his breast
    Like prison'd waters swell.

And feelings, which around his heart
    Had long inertly slept,
Awoke and sway'd the strong, stern man,
    Till he raised his voice and wept.

And he who 'midst his countless wrongs
    Could still undaunted be,
With more than woman's weakness felt
    The weight of being free.

THE SLAVE.

O ! no such blessings on our isle
   Can War's bad triumphs bring,
As these sweet tears, which from the eyes
   Of man enfranchised spring.

And when our might shall melt away,
   And wealth desert our strand,
Within the freeman's chainless breast
   Our monument shall stand.

What though the waves that wash our shore,
   No golden freight may bear ;
The good shall flock from every land,
   And tread in worship there,

And ne'er shall man, whilst in the mind
   Stands Freedom's tenure good,
Forget that on our sainted soil
   Her holiest altar stood.

NIGHTSHADE.

AST by yon hills that brace the glowing
West,
   I watch the sun descend ; his upward
ray
Poised on their rocky tops, he rests awhile,
And lights earth's purple fringe with lacing gold.
Small clouds, like islands in some sleeping sea,
Float high in heaven—motionless, and bathed
In many a hue, as red gives place to red
Still deep'ning ; and the Night steps silent on
Across the waning limits of the Day.
Now comes the quiet moon upon the scene,
Shining, with mellow light, in on the sense,
And glist'ning on the solitary mere.

The willows wave their dark plumes on the bank,
And gentle surges rippling through the reeds,
Mix with the low note of the water-bird.

Here rests tired Nature from her work of day,
And with her stillness calms this anxious heart;
Lets memory of old times come back again,
And the sweet throng of ever pensive thoughts,
And from their depths, those springs that dim the
　　eye.
O! Thou, who broodest in approachless state,
Behind thy temple's blue, impeding veil,
Unseen—alone with thought—the while in turn
Watch at its outward gate pale, trembling stars;
Thou, who can'st make the glare of gorgeous day,
Fade thus insensibly and melt in eve,
Sinking the weary world to gradual rest;
Lord, when my parting hour be come, make me
Feel but the easy slant of natural change,

And that deep quiet which foretells the night :

Make life's descending sun illume all clouds,

And flush my mortal sky with gladd'ning tints,

And then for ever with o'erflooding beams,

Wash the wide landscape from my eyes in light.

O ! when the fires which warm this breast grow
    cold,

Quick may my passage be from light to dark,

And through short twilight to an endless day.

THE FREE CITY OF CRACOW.

—+—

WHAT cry is that which, sad and low,
 Rides upon the swelling gale?
Sad and low and wildly fitful,
 As some spirits' stifled wail.
O! my erring fellow-men!
Know ye not that cry again?

Yes, you know it, 'tis a nation
 Calling, with her latest breath,
On the lands which coldly watch her
 Sink into eternal death;
Starting still some coward doubt,
Whilst her last spark flickers out.

Shall we stand and see these tyrants
  Treading out a people's life ?
Never ! let us plant the standard,
  Draw the brand and dare the strife.
A strength which despots vainly seek
Nerves the arm that shields the weak.

Peace is good, and God has blest it,
  But He never bade the slave
Wither, through a long oppression,
  From the cradle to the grave.
Shall we, for some drops of blood,
Fail to make man's freedom good ?

Come ! my friends, and thou, my country,
  Leave awhile the search for gold ;
Let us march to battle, banded
  For the feeble, as of old.
Yea, since God has will'd it so,
Let us march upon the foe.

CRACOW.

Come! the old heroic legions
　France and England raise again,
And forget your ancient hatred,
　In the common cause of men.
Come! and show the callous Czar
What it is when freemen war.

Would, O! would, one voice might issue
　From the thousand throats of earth,
Rousing nations with its summons
　To a new and grander birth.
Poland! thou at last should'st rest,
Thy bleeding wounds should all be dress'd

Shouts should wake thee from thy stupor,
　Strong arms break thy chains away,
Bear thee swiftly from thy dungeon
　To the golden light of day.
In the darker times of yore
Men have done such deeds before.

Priceless hearts should then be round thee,
Kind hands chafe thy stiffened reins ;
Blood be drawn from glowing manhood
To inject thy stagnant veins.
Then thy wounded soul might see
Peace and tranquil liberty.

THE LINDEN TREE.

"THERE is Death in the house,"

    The old man said ;

    " Death in the house,

  " He is dead ! he is dead !

  " Lead me into the sun,

  " By the linden tree ;

  " For near him now

  " O ! I like not to be."

Then we led him forth

To the sunshine bright,

To the garden seat,

Where he sat till night ;

His face to the sun,
His hands on his knees,
And his white hair blown
By the passing breeze.
And he kept, whilst Death
Was under the roof,
As long as he might
From the house aloof.

The fifth day came
Since the spirit had passed
From his youthful son—
His first and his last.
The fifth day came,
And the summons fell
From the iron tongue
Of the burial bell.
Then we bound his hat
With the dark crape shade,

And his form
In a funeral cloak arrayed.
As he sat so still
By his favourite tree,
And gazed on the death-pomp
Unconsciously.
Not a sign of grief
Or feeling he gave,
As we led him on
To his firstborn's grave,
But eyed the dark train
As it wended there,
With a glassy eye
And a vacant stare.

O! slowly we go
With the cherished one,
To a tearful scene
Which has but begun ;

We hear, but heed not,

The words of the priest,

Which must fall from lips

Ere the worms can feast ;

For our thoughts lie beneath

Yon mantled bier,

Where Death clasps the clay

That we held so dear.

Then forth from the church

Take our mournful way,

Whilst the sighing winds

With the green leaves play ;

The flowers, the bright heaven,

He cannot see,

Giving sharper edge

To our misery ;

Till we stand by the cramp'd

And hollow space,

They have clear'd in the ground
For his resting-place.
Then rude hands fasten
The cords to his shell,
Sling it and lower it
Into its cell ;
Heave the black damp earth
On its rattling lid,
Till its bright plate and planks
Of oak are hid ;
And duller and duller
A sullen sound,
Comes from the mould
They pile up and around.

All is done ; then, why
Does the old man stay ?
We ask him to come,
He will not away ;

For his eye is tracing,

Beneath that heap,

A form swathed and rigid

And locked in sleep ;

Tracing the features,

So rayless and white,

Once lit up by love

And the mind's clear light ;

And the curls which cling

To the clammy brow ;

And the bound-up jaws

Which are nerveless now ;

And the sunken eye,

And the hollow cheek,

And the shrivelled lips

Which have ceased to speak.

There he sees him again,

As he lay on the bed,

In the cold frost that rivets
The blood of the dead.

All is done! all is done!
But the old man stands,
And wrings in wildness
His withered hands ;
And the waves of grief
Pent up in his breast
Are rising and falling
And give no rest.
His heart is torn,
And we see from his air,
How deeply the iron
Must have entered there.
Then we tear him away
From the closing grave,
To the gate where the plumes
Of the death-coach wave :

And we lead him, in tears,

Through the quiet lane,

Till he stands on the threshold

Of home again.

And now in the warm light

He still loves to be,

As he thinks of his son

By the linden tree.

THE LIFE-STREAM.

—✦—

ROM shadow to twilight,
   · From slumber to dream,
  From deadness to being,
    Flows out the life-stream.
With the sound of a tongue
  On the palate and lips
Through a long dripping cavern
  It oozily slips.
Like a snake through the thin grass,
  It winds and it weaves;
On its banks the trees huddle
  With shivering leaves.
Its black swirling masses
  Slow oceanward swing;

Aloft flaps the raven
   His quill-creaking wing.
We are born, we are plunged
   Into life's gloomy river;
The cold wave receives us,
   Then closes for ever.
On the face of the waters
   A shouting is heard,
The air for a moment
   Above them is stirred;
But ere the first sound-wave
   Breaks sad by the shore,
The voice which impelled it
   Is ringing no more.
Awhile on the surface
   A bubble is seen,
The breath of a mortal,
   It bursts—he has been.

THE TRULY BRAVE.

THOUGH no fresh laurels deck the grave
Which closes o'er the truly brave,
The brave, who in defence of right,
From youth till age undaunted fight ;
And Fame disdainful pass the dust
Which shrouds the relics of the just :
Think not from earth unpaid depart
The men of mind, the great of heart.
Their life's deep stream flows smoothly on,
Calm in its course of duties done,
The poet's praise, the patriot's tear,
Shall grace in death their modest bier.

SONNET.

TO AN EARLY FRIEND.

—•—

T is not with us as it was in youth ;

    Sleep falls not now upon our languid

    sight,

Soft as a shadow from the wing of night ;

And gladness has not grown along with truth.

Ye fond illusions of our earlier day !

    Visions ! that came from out the field of thought

    In joyous troops, fast flocking and unsought !

Still as we live, ye leave us on the way.

And yet, though care is crowding on content,

    Though Reason claims her painful sacrifice,

And ever sadder makes, to make more wise;
Say why should'st thou, should I, my friend, lament,
Since that strong stay amidst the wreck has stood,
Which keeps unshaken still our faith in good.

EPITAPH.

Y E who can worth and manliness admire,
A generous nature, true poetic fire ;
Freshness of heart not oft surviving youth,
A mind expansive and a soul all truth ;
A hand that gave, yet knew not how to take,
An independence misery could not break ;
A prudent frankness, spirits ever gay,
That lit even blindness with a steady ray ;
Sense, courage, virtue, all combined to form
The noblest breastwork against life's rude storm :
Turn on this simple stone no careless eye,
For here the ashes of a just man lie,

Who strove to free the thought from bigot rules,

Imposed by tyrants and upheld by fools;

And claimed for all mankind their rights as men,

By daring converse and a vigorous pen.

THE DEATH OF SALE.

—◆—

THE warrior has fallen, how calm is his rest,
Where he sleeps on the bed which a
soldier loves best !
No sickness distressed him, no lengthened decay,
In the arms of no weepers his life pass'd away ;
But the rough sea of battle swell'd high by his side,
And the soul of the hero went forth on its tide.

They are bearing in silence the noble, the brave,
To his home in the darkness and depth of the grave ;
The flag he so cherished waves torn by his bier,
The men whom he led, and who loved him are near.
Their strong voices falter, their eyes are all dim,
As they speak their last blessing—"God's rest be
on him !"

And O! though their leader be nerveless and cold,

Though his shout sound no more, which inspired
them of old,

Whilst his spirit survives, whilst it breathes in the
field,

Though match'd against thousands no Briton shall
yield.

Nor stain by defeat, till the streams of life fail,

The banner which waved o'er the last home of Sale.

VALEDICTION.

WHEN last, my father, in the crowd of men,
  With but the words which custom
    wills, we parted,
I stayed to gaze upon thy form again,
 And half to greet thee more in love I started.

I gazed, till partly in the haze of tears,
 And partly in the thronging mass it faded,
Then turned upon myself, and with my fears
 For thee, I made a veil which all things shaded.

Yet wherefore tears ? Though in this sordid strife
 Thy noble mind hath been but ill-respected ;
Wherefore ? Though lately in the close of life
 By meaner hearts thy heart hath been neglected.

Heed not, though only to thyself be known,

 And to the faithful few, thine inward story ;

What thou hast felt, shall bring thee near His throne,

 Who weaves the wreath of all immortal glory.

And O ! my father, wilt thou, when the soul,

 Which now some glorious impulse ever swayeth,

Starts from its shell, and freed from low control,

 Fast by the pure and true, in calmness strayeth,

Look forth upon thy son from that clear height,

 Still in this vale of tears and darkness dwelling,

Speak to his spirit in the deep of night,

 To deeds like thine and love like thine impelling?

GARIBALDI ENTERS LONDON.

OH ! who is he, who clad in gray,
    By bridge and tower and palace gate,
    Through gathering thousands makes his
        way,
Secure, serene, supremely great,
Yea, greater far than crowned king,
Amidst a people triumphing ?

No orders deck his generous breast,
    No victor laurel binds his brow,
And yet in virtue simply dressed,
    He mocks the stateliest monarch now.
Oh ! who is he, so proudly led ?
'Tis Garibaldi, call'd the " Red."

So was the Spartan warrior red,

    Borne homeward on his brassy shield,

And patriot Hampden when he bled,

    For English rights, on Chalgrove field ;

Red with the fight's ensanguined sea,

Red with thy blood, O! Liberty.

Then friends and lovers greet him well

    With feast and song and joyous laugh,

With every toast that tongue can tell,

    The crimson wine in welcome quaff.

Pledge him, ye Britons, hand to hand,

And when he leaves our sea-girt land,

Waft him, ye winds, across the wave

    Straight onward to his island home,

Soon from the Gallic grasp to save

    Thy seven hills, O! ruined Rome,

Soon, soon to write, as Cæsar wrote—

I came, I saw, I conquering smote.

O! breath of song, how vain to break

    The might of sword-encircled kings!

Can all the verse that poets make,

    Disarm the legions Gallia brings?

Can Reason rend the fatal chain

Which weighs on men where bayonets reign?

CAUBUL.

HERE is a manliness in real grief,

That courts no sympathy, seeks no relief,

That will not shame the Dead with vain
regret,

Nor the white Urn with vainer weeping wet :

Yet still can cherish in the faithful heart,

Of those no more, the best, the noblest part ;

Not the faint impress of the form or face

Which Time's rude hand may rapidly erase,

But that grand fabric Nature leaves behind,

The imperishable image of the mind ;

Still can each deed, each generous thought recall,

And spur the soul to emulate them all.

This is true Honor to departed worth,

Not the weak tears that Sorrow sheds on Earth.

Let women weep, for us more sternly bred

Enough if those who die be nobly dead ;

If o'er them stream'd the flag they bled to save,

Their mourners men, a field of fame their grave !

    Thus on the brave should fond remembrance dwell,

The brave, who low in death, by Caubul fell,

When Fortune failed them, and reverses came

To soil the chaplet of our Indian Fame.

Nor theirs the fault : for base inaction broke

Their once high souls beneath its sluggard yoke,

Though Affghan guile around, and from afar

The crafty Scythian, fann'd the flame of war,

Till dread rebellion o'er th' affrighted land

With frantic gesture shook her crimson hand.

    'Tis well in Peril's darkest hour to find,

Prompt for each turn of Fate, some master-mind,

Safe in success, in danger undismayed,
By no rash heat, no shallow counsel swayed ;
Whose piercing vision sees through every cloud
That wraps with impotence the duller crowd.
Though all be lost and viler souls despair,
Imperial reason keeps her station there ;
Rallies the·broken ranks with skilful hand,
And whilst one file remains shall yet command :
For instinct-led the weaker nature still
Clings, like a parasite, round stronger will,
And still for Hope amidst the battle's brunt
Seeks the keen eye, the calm impassive front.
But no such spirit stay'd their wavering course,
Gave strength to weakness, or design to force.
A feeble chief his sacred trust betrayed,
For foul retreat the fatal compact made,
Hired savage hordes by deepest treachery stain'd
To rescue men whilst yet the sword remain'd ;

Men whose firm hearts are never known to claim

A safety purchased by their country's shame!

Long o'er Jellallabad, heroic Sale,

Thy spotless standard braved the adverse gale:

Herat, Ghuznee, and many a field attest

A Spartan valour warms the British breast!

Lo! as the Day-God fading on the view

His last faint radiance from the landscape drew;

Wrapp'd in repose, and voiceless as the clay

By life no more illumed, the City lay:

No sound disturbs the stillness of the camp,

Save the lone sentinel's unceasing tramp:

Not one glad heart amidst that drooping throng

Breaks the deep night-spell by the charm of song;

No echo, wakening from her couch of reeds,

In playful cadence on its music feeds.

And once again, before their last long rest,

By famine wasted and by toil oppress'd,

Their heavy lids with slumber's signet sealed,

England's rude sons have sunk upon the field.

And there, too, sleeps the fairer fragile form,

That ill may meet the madness of the storm ;

Yet woman's frame of Nature's softest cast

Can brave, and bloom amidst the raging blast,

Like the pale flower whose sweets the tempests rear,

The snow-nurs'd offspring of the youthful year !

Parent of Elde ! these are thy children all,

Must they ignobly and for ever fall ?

Earth's faded plants shall know another Spring,

To other years refreshened beauty bring :

But ne'er may man, the great, the good, the wise

From her cold lap to second being rise,

Till thy dread mandate fill the depths of space,

And Time and Nature close upon his race.

When shall he then from each base impulse turn,

Thy plain intent, thy simple lesson learn ?

Learn from the seas of blood by conquest shed,
From the false hues o'er glory's bubble spread,
From nations wasted, kingdoms passed away,
From the soul's servage, and the thought's decay;
That mind, might, empire all at last must prove
But shadowy phantoms to thy truth of Love.

Soon as the clear note of the bugle-horn
Rings through the frosted panoply of morn,
Forth from the gaping breach and portal wide
In lengthened volume rolls the living tide.
Onward till eve, in march confused and slow,
Toiling a passage through the drifted snow,
The vanguard near the pass; an awful gloom,
A lurid darkness haunts their destined tomb;
Upon whose verge the boldest hearts grow chill
With the vague presage of approaching ill,
As fast around their rearward columns close
The myriad legions of avenging foes.

'Tis done! the doom'd band treads the deadly path
Planted with secret ministers of wrath!
Sudden on high the echoing volleys ring,
From every rock the ambush'd traitors spring:
The shock of battle, and the deafening sound
Of charging squadrons rend the air around.
And lo! where bursts the tempest of the fight,
Where iron death-showers wing their withering flight,
Beaten to earth, the wounded masses writhe;
Rank falls on rank like grass beneath the scythe.
When morn's faint beamings, from the leaden east,
Shine o'er the lazy Vulture's sickening feast,
In ghastly heaps the dying and the dead
Shall tell how fearfully those rebels sped.
Forth from the Pass a shattered remnant came
That toil had crush'd not, terror could not tame;
Slowly with reeling step the gallant band
Pants up yon hill to make a farewell stand.

There hunted, worn, of countless hosts the prey,

Grimly the British Warrior stood at bay.

Then pealed aloft his startling battle-cry,

Thrill'd through the frame and gave it strength to die ;

No weak resolve, no sordid sigh for life

Dimm'd the bright lustre of that parting strife :

The foot advanced, the eye upon the foe,

With failing life-streams fainter fell each blow,

Till the proud heart sent forth its latest breath

And own'd no victor but resistless Death !

Nerveless those sinewy limbs, the dark orbs closed,

The bosom cold where manly faith reposed,

And feeble now that pulseless breast to move

The spell of genius or the dream of love :

Never again upon his ear shall beat

The soul's fresh welcome, nor the converse sweet

Of her who once around his strong form hung,

Love's broken accents faltering on her tongue,

With heart too sad her mingled thoughts to speak,
The big drops gathering on her pallid cheek ;
For full and deep the springs of feeling lie
That dim, yet show so fair in, woman's eye ;
And still 'midst joy and hope some latent fear
Calls from its holy font the glist'ning tear.

Such is War's costly offering, and the Prize
That conquerors clutch, a Human Sacrifice.

Far from their Isle that crowns the western deep
The perished heroes of our country sleep.
O'er them awhile the insulting foe may tread,
May spurn with dastard heel the mighty dead,
Awhile rejoice, but Summer's sun shall bring
The fierce Avenger for his reckoning.
In vain revenge : around their lonely grave
May springing flow'rs in wild luxuriance wave ;
And there—as Surya sheds his parting ray
O'er purpled plain and mountains far away,

E

Till Evening's sombre shadows stealing on
Blend his rich hues, his thousand tints in one:
When the fresh wind, whose fitful breathing weaves
A viewless pathway through the rustling leaves,
Mellowed by distance, yet though distant clear,
Wafts waves of music to the listening ear—
When, in the stilly air, the soft dews weep,
The Muse of Memory shall her vigils keep.
Sadness and feeling beaming from her eye
That seeks in ecstacy the radiant sky,
Where, in the vast void to the goal of sight,
Mysterious systems speed upon their flight.
As back from them her own deep gaze is given,
Too bright for earth, too full of earth for heav'n,
Thus shall her voice its solemn silence break,
And, tuned to melody, in wisdom speak.

   "When first from Chaos dark this stately world
" By force Almighty into space was hurl'd,

" The germs of Beauty locked within its breast,

" No forms of loveliness of grace express'd ;

" But ages passing to their ocean, Time,

" Saw Nature labouring in pangs sublime,

" Till, amidst throes of pain and wearing strife,

" From her old frame came forth a fairer life,

" And wooed to being by more genial skies,

" Verdure, and fragrance her rich incense rise.

" So, by that force, these wretched scenes may prove

" But the dark process through which life must move;

" Ere, as the storm-clouds slowly roll away,

" That great conception sees a brighter day

" Stain'd by no wars, by no oppressions cursed,

" To heavenly aims in manly virtue nursed :

" When lust and rapine shall no more be known,

" And freedom call the sons of earth her own.

   " There is a Temple meant for every man,

" Fenced by no partial, no proscribing ban,

" Whose glorious structure, of immortal birth,

" Looms grandly o'er the palaces of Earth.

" Ample for all that live its vast embrace,

" 'Tis the Love-Spirit's mystic dwelling-place !

" Beneath its canopy o'ershadowing all

" Let gathered nations prone in worship fall ;

"Let them, O God ! from brute-like passions cease,

" And work in lasting links the chain of PEACE !"

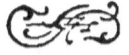

THE GOLDEN CHAIN.

—♦—

THERE are two kinds of men on earth,
　　The men who have, and have to get ;
　　Wealth is the test which tries our worth,
　A rude, a vulgar one—and yet
Under its action all are brought,
The foolish and the full of thought.

To reach the sphere where that is found,
　　The dull aspire, the bright descend ;
God will'd that on some common ground
　　Mankind should seek a common end ;
And thus by mingling heart with heart
He better makes the baser part.

Those see in wealth life's solid prize,
    The aim of toil, the end of care ;
But these, whilst in the strife, despise
    The ignoble spoil which brings them there ;
Yet virtue without gold is vain,
And genius must contend with gain.

O ! happy he who in that fight
    The freshness of the heart can keep,
Whom simple pleasures still delight,
    Who still can smile and still can weep ;
Where minds are soured and hopes are cross'd,
And faith and feeling often lost.

And O ! thrice happy if away
    From toil and tumult, freed at times,
His spirit leave its casing clay,
    And circle heavenward weaving rhymes,
And find within thought's spreading zone
Fresh orbs which fancy makes his own.

For to the head and to the heart,
　Which meaning from the world can wring,
There is a sense in every part,
　A latent good in every thing :
The music-lines of Nature's plan
Are fair to read and plain to scan.

But on the man of narrow mind
　Her harmony is thrown away ;
The clouds which his perception bind
　Are never broken up by day ;
He leaves no foot-prints in the land,
No tide-mark on life's shifting sand.

The fitness of the perfect whole,
　The constant aim, the hidden charm,
The pulse which beats through all, the soul,
　Which keeps the springs of being warm ;
He sees not, heeds not,—in his eyes
But to be rich is to be wise.

Self is the basis of his creed,
　　The centre of his low desire ;
The plants of which God sows the seed
　　Within his barren breast expire ;
As through a mist, before his glass,
The earth's bright visions dimly pass.

He lives, he loves ; but what a life !
　　A feverish panting after gain,
He hardens in the fruitless strife,
　　And dying feels he lived in vain.
Yes ; when his shell of wealth is cast,
The voice within him speaks at last.

He loves ; but, no, the source of love
　　Lies not imprisoned far below ;
'Tis not the spring whose wave above
　　Its dark well-wall can never flow,
Which, loth to give and slow to rise,
Within a selfish circle dies.

Love is a fount whose gushing yields
　　The volume of a noble river,
Which by the town and through the fields,
　　With deep'ning bed rolls on for ever ;
Ending its gifts but with its flood,
Its passion with its power for good.

Love is a ray to tinge each cloud,
　　Which threats life's summer day with shade ;
Love is a flower which in our shroud
　　A hand we cannot press has laid :
A scent which perfumes all it meets,
And wastes itself in giving sweets.

O ! he who has that love so deep,
　　And with it has the nameless force
That will not let his spirit keep
　　The bounds which mark the many's course ;
Who fearless treads the waste of thought
In search of treasures none have sought.

Who sees, as manhood masters youth,
  The splendid braggarts, wealth and birth,
Grow pale before the flag of Truth,
  And perish in the lists with worth,
Who save the wise and good alone,
Will other nobles never own.

O! in his breast the sacred flame,
  The central heat is burning strong;
And glowing thoughts will wrap his frame,
  Until they melt and flow in Song;
Nor long about the precious ore,
The furnace-blast shall vainly roar.

For him the veil of Time is riven,
  The map of destiny unfurl'd;
To him the power to hear is given,
  The mystic voices of the world;
He learns the secret from the seen,
What is to be from what has been.

Aloft on some unsullied height,
  Above the tempest and the cloud,
He trembling waits to greet the light,
  Whilst dark below him sleeps the crowd ;
And fills his soul, in rapture there,
With Nature's immemorial prayer.

Then from afar comes forth a voice,
  A spirit to his spirit calls—
" Fear not and faint not, but rejoice,
  " On thee the prophet-mantle falls ;
" Into its wondrous web are wrought,
" The threads of action and of thought.

" Rejoice ! rejoice ! no base alloy
  " Shall mingle with thy soul again ;
" All, all within thee shall be joy,
  " And light and hope and love of men,
" And tears to fall like gentle rain,
" Upon the arid waste of pain.

" To thee, beneath the tree of life,

　" Whose branches, moaning in the blast,

" Sigh out the lay of human strife,—

　" The story of the far-off past,

" Of ages onward from of old,

" In rustling whispers shall be told.

" And thou shalt sing, but no weak plaint,

　" No bitter words against thy kind ;

" Nor as the thankless race who paint

　" As that of all, their own bad mind,

" Whom Nature places under ban

" As false interpreters to man.

" Thy song shall be a song of praise,

　" For ever upward tend thy soul ;

" As the silk globe which frets and sways

　" And labours to escape control,

" Cut from the cords which check'd its rise,

" Seeks its right level in the skies.

" Like one who from the land's green crest

   " Marks as he gazes on the Deep,—

" Whether the winds have gone to rest,

   " And in its glassy hollows sleep,

" Whilst sounds of waves that rib the beach

" His ear in distant murmurs reach ;

" Or waking at the sea-birds' cry,

   " The furious tempests start and throw

" The gasping ocean to the sky—

   " That still the waters ebb and flow ;

" So thou in life, through calm or storm,

" Shalt trace God's goodness uniform."

SONG.

Air, " PESTAL."

———

ELL ! the dream of old,

   The patriot-hope at last is o'er ;

   And for thee, my land !

This heart will bleed but ache no more.

Now the tyrant may on me his vengeance take,

But those passions strong,

Love and hate of wrong,

Till the fire of life this wasted frame forsake,

He shall never, never break.

Why so sad, my heart !

And why so loth to yield thy breath ?

Wilt thou, wilt thou friend !

Desert me on the march to death ?

Long from sunless vaults for thee, O Liberty !

Firm to meet his God,

Has the martyr trod ;

So will I give unto heaven this spirit free,

Even as it came to me.

Then thou beating heart,

Be still awhile, and with the free,

The holy and the just,

We soon shall be, we soon shall be.

LOSS OF THE TROOP-SHIP
"BIRKENHEAD."

H ! the winds were all at rest,
    There was calm on ocean's breast,
    Not a giant mountain crest
        Broke in spray ;

As the ship along the land,
Scarce a gunshot from the strand,
With a brave and happy band,
    Made her way.

All were resting on the deep,
In the plenitude of sleep,
Save the midnight watch, who keep
    Guard on deck ;

When the steamer, as she sped,
Struck a sunken rock ahead,
And the gallant Birkenhead
Lay a wreck!

For a moment, terror wild
Fell on woman, man and child,
As the waters darkly smiled
Round their prey;

But the captain's hardy shout
Like a trumpet-note rang out,
And soon quelled the rising rout
And dismay.

" Let the boats be quickly manned!
" Then, that wife and child may land,
" Every man on board must stand
" By the ship."

F

There was not a selfish sigh,
Not a tremor of the eye ;
Not a weak, despairing cry
    Left a lip.

They shall land !—across the foam,
They shall hear the bells at home,
In the summer-fields shall roam
    Once again :

Whilst for those they leave behind,
There's a bond by Honour signed,
And a grave, which Fame shall find
    On the main.

Then the weak ones down the side,
Like pale phantoms seem to glide
To the boats which safely ride
    On the lee.

Soon the deck asunder parts ;
Stand fast ye valiant hearts !
Not a timid traitor starts
    Towards the sea.

For the soldiers undismayed,
In their silent ranks arrayed,
Sank, upon their last parade,
    Sternly down ;

And the sailors, as they stood,
In their fearless northern mood,
Settled with them, in the flood,
    To renown.

Then, like God's own minstrelsy,
Rose the anthem of the sea,
As its countless waves of glee
    Softly sound ;

Whilst the Sirens, in their cave,
Spread a banquet for the brave,
Where the coral branches wave
    All around.

In the battle's red eclipse,
In the death-embrace of ships,
At the cannon's iron lips,
    What is breath ?

But 'tis courage bright and high,
When the yawning waves are nigh,
To look forth with dauntless eye
    Upon death.

At the muster of all hands
Which high Heaven itself commands,
When that brave battalion stands
    To its arms ;

What a Glory round each face
Shall the hands of angels trace,
What sweet words of praise efface
    All alarms!

Not alone by duties done
'Midst the thunders of the gun,
Is the crown of Valour won
    For a State;

There are bloodless deeds which rise
Like fine incense to the skies,
Where the saints in Paradise
    Hail the great.

What fear for England then,
When from shore to mountain glen
Such a peerless race of men
    Rise in might?

Let the tyrants of an hour,
When the clouds of battle lower,
Learn to dread a Briton's power
In the fight.

LONDON :
PRINTED BY CHARLES WESTERTON,
27, ST. GEORGE'S PLACE, HYDE PARK CORNER.